christmas with the monster

sabrina cross

For all of the friends I made on the bird app. Thanks for over a decade of amusement, entertainment, and support. Y'all are directly to blame for this.

one

. . .

WAS THERE anything more depressing than an empty house on Christmas Eve? The tree was decked out with garland, tinsel, and baubles. Twinkling lights flashed in the windows, coffee filter snowflakes hung from the ceiling. Stockings lined in a neat row on the mantle.

The house was ready for Christmas to arrive, but I sure as fuck wasn't.

"I still can't believe that twig-dicked asshole did this." My best friend Amy's voice carried through the quiet room as she ranted through the phone. "He's never once cared about the holidays or visitation before and now suddenly it's vital he gets them Christmas Eve? The least he could do is drop them off after dinner so they could do the morning at home, where they belong."

"He's worried about the weather." I stared out the window at the dark, cloudy sky. There was snow in the forecast, but not until late in the night. There was no rational reason my ex couldn't have brought the kids home after dinner with his family. No reason other than he was a twig-dicked asshole.

"It's not even supposed to start snowing until

late tonight. He's just being an asshole." I lifted my glass of wine in salute to my phone, which sat on the arm of the couch, before taking a drink. "Are you sure you don't want me to come over? Ethan is decorating cookies with the kids."

"I'm sure. I'm going to lay here, drink some wine, maybe watch a holiday movie or two."

"Black Christmas is not a Christmas movie."

"Sure it is, it's right there in the name." I took another drink of my wine and picked up the remote. "Go be the picture-perfect family. Send me actual pictures. We'll see you Saturday."

"Okay, but call me if you change your mind."

"I will. I promise." I wouldn't be calling her. And I wouldn't change my mind. Amy would absolutely drive across town to sit with me, but I had no interest in sharing my misery. It wasn't her fault I chose to have kids with a jerk. Or said jerk's parents were in town for Christmas and wanted to see the kids, forcing the jerkface to demand visitation. Funny, he knew it was technically his Christmas with the kids, despite not taking them the last five years.

"I mean it, Devynn. Call me if you need me." She was using her mom voice on me.

"I swear to Santa Claus, I will call you if I need anything." I settled on a horror movie, not Black Christmas, and queued it up. "I love you, bye.

"I love you, bye."

I hung up the phone and poured another glass of wine from the bottle on my side table. I grabbed the popcorn and settled in for a long night of streaming movies and trying not to be miserable about not having my kids on the most magical holiday of the year.

two

. . .

IT WAS the sound of breaking glass that woke me. Not a loud crash like a window or the patio door, but the tinkle of a bulb falling to the ground. My first thought was the kids had snuck downstairs early. But no, the kids were with their dad.

I grabbed my phone and checked the time. Just after midnight. Merry Christmas, Devynn, someone broke into your house and is breaking your ornaments. I sat in bed listening for another sound, but it was silent. The heater was running, but there were no other sounds to be heard. Maybe the vent had blown a lighter bulb off the tree?

The smartest thing to do would probably have been call the cops or someone to come check out the house. But I didn't want to look like a crazy person if they showed up and I was alone with no signs of a break-in besides the broken bulb.

"Okay girl, you've got this. There's no one in the house. It was just the heater." I wasn't very convincing.

Still, I wasn't a total moron. I grabbed the softball bat left over from my high school days from behind the bedroom door and slid my phone into the pocket of my shorts. If nothing else, throwing it at them might give me time to lock myself in the bathroom so I could call the cops.

Plan, as idiotic as it may have been, in place, I left the bedroom as silently as I could. The wood floor creaked under my feet. Had it always been so loud? I mentally cursed myself for buying the old house the entire trip down the hall.

Still, there was no movement or noise. I pressed myself close to the wall and creeped my way down the hallway toward the front of the house.

The lights still twinkled in the living room, giving me flashes of bright white light followed by moments of darkness. The whole effect was unsettling. But as I got closer to the living room, my fear started to abate. I was probably being crazy. It was my first time alone in the house in months and I was probably just hearing things. There was absolutely no one in the house with me.

Nothing, not a single damn thing in my life, could have prepared me for the sight waiting for me in my living room.

There, in the middle of my living room, stealing the presents from under the tree, was a tall, furry, green monster.

I did the only thing any sane person would do in that situation. I started laughing. I was clearly drunk and hallucinating. It was the only possible reason for the furry green giant with a dad bod standing naked in my living room. He wore nothing but a red Santa hat.

He spun around at my laughter.

"Well, hello there." His voice was gruff and harsh, like someone who hadn't spoken in a long while.

"What the fuck do you think you're doing?"

three

...

THE MONSTER GAVE ME A GRIN, a flash of white teeth against green flesh and fur. He gave a little bow in my direction.

"Why, I'm here to fix your tree." He gestured to the large pine beside him. "Did you not notice there is a light out on it?"

I instinctively moved forward to look for the burnt-out bulb. There hadn't been one the night before. My tree had been perfect and ready for the kids to get home and enjoy.

It was a mistake.

The second I was within reach, the green monster grabbed me by my arm. He spun me until my back pressed against his front, both of my arms trapped between our bodies. He wrapped an arm around my upper chest and pinned me into place.

"Mmmm, I caught myself a pretty," he mumbled into my hair. He inhaled a deep breath, taking in my scent. "Are you a good girl or a naughty girl, pretty?"

Shame filled me as my stomach quivered. I was absolutely not getting turned on by being pinned against the tall creature. Even if he was firm against my back. And warm. And the sound of his rusty voice was shooting straight through my body.

Even if I hadn't been with anyone in years. I definitely didn't have a praise kink a mile wide getting off on the idea of being called a good girl in that unused voice. I didn't at all imagine he was speaking only for me.

"Let me go!" I struggled against him. Against myself. "Please, let me go. I'll pretend I never saw you, you can steal someone else's presents."

"I'm not here for the presents, pretty." The arm clasped across my upper chest moved down until his large hand pressed against my soft belly. He moved me back against his body until I could feel every inch of him.

"I'll let you go," his hard cock pressed into my back. A cock that hadn't been there when I first saw him. I definitely would have noticed it…

His mouth came down to lick the base of my neck where it met my shoulder. "If that's really what you want.

"But you see, I think you're a naughty girl who tries so hard to be good. I think a naughty girl like you doesn't want me to leave." He ground his hips into me and bit my neck. A cry burst from my lips. It wasn't pain, god help me, but pleasure that coursed through my entire body. "I think a naughty girl like you wants to be my good girl and take whatever I give you."

His large, furry green hand trailed lower on my belly, stopping short of my pussy. The traitorous thing was throbbing with the need to be touched. My hands were now tangled in the fur on his firm, round belly. I was holding him to me as much as he held me to him.

"Please," I begged, but even I wasn't sure what I

was begging for anymore. My entire body was a live wire, electric and pulled taut. Fear clawed at my throat while pure lust throbbed through me.

"Just tell me what you want, pretty." His fingers curled around the curve of my belly, tips pressing into the top of my mound. I bit back a moan. "Tell the Imp what you want and I'll give it to you."

"This is insane. Impossible." I shook my head against his shoulder. He nipped at my neck.

"It's Christmas, pretty. Anything is possible." His fingers inched lower, not touching, but ghosting over my wanting flesh. "Though I will admit to being a touch insane. But that doesn't scare a naughty girl like you."

He released his grip on my arms and brought his other hand up to rest against my throat. My pulse was racing and I flushed, knowing he could feel it. Knowing he wouldn't write it off as fear. Because he knew what I was.

I was a nasty, naughty girl and I was wildly turned on by this creature.

"Touch me." The words were a whisper, barely able to come out through the pressure of his hand on my throat. "Please."

"Mmm, there's the good girl I knew was in there. So polite." His hand slid down and cupped me through my cotton sleep shorts. Long fingers pressed between my folds to circle my throbbing clitoris and I couldn't bite back the sob of aching need.

The hand at my neck applied pressure to force my head back until I was looking into the creature's yellow eyes. They immediately locked onto my gaze and something burned there, a fever that frightened me as much as it aroused me.

"Is this what you want, pretty?" A slow circle

around my clit, just enough stimulation to make me jerk, but nowhere near enough to get me off. "I can give you so much more, you just need to ask."

There was a demand in his eyes. A promise. I stood frozen, staring at him, his hand still against my neck, the other pressed against my pleasure button.

I wasn't the type of person to have a one-night stand. I never had a ho phase in college or after my divorce. I hadn't ever been a candidate for Girls Gone Wild. It had been years since I'd last tried dating and longer still since I'd had a satisfying sexual experience.

Something about the green monster screamed he knew exactly what he was doing and would enjoy every moment of it. His cock twitched against my back and I ground back into it without thinking. The movement pressed his finger into my button, making me squirm against him for more friction.

Yes, it was insane, but I was going to fuck the monster. And I was certain I would enjoy every moment of it.

four

· · ·

IN FOR A PENNY, in for a pound.

When the creature released me and told me to strip, I wasted no time listening. He helped me remove my robe, shorts, and t-shirt, his furry hands brushing against every inch of skin we exposed. They were a strange sensation, soft but coarse. They tickled my flesh and made me squirm in his grasp as they traveled across over-sensitized skin.

"So pretty," he moved behind me again, pressing me back against his cock with a hand around the curve of my belly. His other hand cupped and squeezed my breast. Long fingers with thick, black nails pinched at my nipple.

I arched into his touch, eager for whatever he would give me. I wanted to beg, plead, demand. I wanted more. And more was what he gave me.

His hand slid south, parting my lower lips, and slid into the moist channel between them. He brushed over my clit before sliding down to tease at my opening. Again and again, he followed the slow path from my aching, dripping hole and my swollen, throbbing clit. All the while, his other hand squeezed and pinched at my breast.

"Such a good girl, getting so wet for me." His fingertip dipped inside and I thrust down toward him, not getting enough and needing so much more. He teased and tormented, but offered no relief or release. My entire body was taut with pleasure, teetering on the edge but not getting enough to go over.

"You're such a fucking tease," I whined while I tried to grind against his hand.

"Oh, you shouldn't have said that." His voice was low, amused. He pulled away from me and went to get a large red sack I hadn't noticed under the tree.

"I take it back." I slid my hand between my thighs toward my aching cunt, but he was there in a flash, grabbing my wrist and pulling it away.

"Uh, uh, uh, no touching." He drew my hand behind my back before grabbing the other one. He grasped my wrists in one large hand and reached into the sack. "Now, are you going to be a good girl?"

Gold flashed in the corner of my eye and I craned my neck to see him with a roll of gold ribbon. It was wrapping paper ribbon, the kind meant to curl with the blade of the scissors. He deftly unrolled part of it with one hand before he began wrapping it around my wrist.

My heart shot into my throat and I began to struggle against his hold. With one move, he knocked my feet out from under me and laid me face down on the carpet. He straddled my back and pinned my arms behind me.

He leaned down until his chest was against my arms and back so he could speak into my ear.

"Be a good girl and stop struggling. Such a naughty girl, trying to touch without permission."

"I'm sorry," I murmured into the floor. My breath was coming in harsh pants and I fought to slow my heart from racing. "Please don't."

"The choice is yours, pretty." Ribbon trailed along my side, tickling my skin. "I can stop now and send you back to bed. Or you can let me have my way with you and I'll give you everything you want and things you've never even dreamed about."

The clock ticked on the mantle as silence fell. It was my choice. Was I crazy enough to let the furry green monster tie me up and leave me helpless?

"Say yes, pretty." He trailed a dull nail up my side, teasing the side of my breast before sliding under me to pinch the nipple. "Say yes, and let me make you feel better than you've ever felt before. I've got a bit of Christmas magic in my sack and I'll use it all on you."

He pulled his hand free and moved it up to circle my neck. His cock perfectly lined up against the crease of my ass and he slowly ground it back and forth against me. It was hard and throbbing and felt impossibly big.

"I can make you feel so good. And all you have to do is say yes." He bit the side of my neck, blunt teeth sinking into sensitive skin and sending a pulse of sensation through my body.

"Yes!" The word was a sob and a prayer.

"Mmm, good girl." The monster sat up, still straddling my hips. The gold ribbon quickly wrapped around and between my wrists, securing my arms in place. Once tied off, the rest of the roll was tossed to the side.

He rose off of me and reached down to grab me. Two large hands on my upper arms hauled me to my feet.

"Now, you were a naughty girl and naughty girls need to be punished. But don't worry pretty, you'll like what I do to you." The monster sat before jerking me forward to lay across his lap. One hand came down on my back, holding me in place. Before I could even fully process the position, a hand came down sharply on my ass.

I yelped in equal parts surprise and pain. I hadn't been spanked since I was a small child and the humiliation of that experience flooded through me. I struggled against him, but he held me firmly in position.

"You can stop this at any time. But once you say the word, I'll leave. Do you understand?"

I nodded my head. I understood and while the position was humiliating, my clit still throbbed and my pussy clenched around nothing. I needed release and this wasn't so terrible.

"Use your words, pretty."

"I understand." The words were a whisper. It was apparently enough to satisfy him. The next thing I knew his hand came down again, smacking against my naked skin. I couldn't help but cry out.

"No, no, we can't have that." The monster leaned forward and grabbed his red sack. "That won't do at all."

He dropped the sack on my back and rummaged through it. I wriggled beneath its weight, but he kept his other hand pinning me in place.

"Ah-ha!" He pulled something from the sack and dropped the bag on the couch by my feet. "Open."

I did so without thought. Something pressed between my lips and I instinctively bit down. The taste of peppermint filled my taste buds as the candy cane began to melt in my mouth.

"Don't let it drop." His hand rubbed against my ass, soft fur and leathery flesh setting off a fire inside of me. While I tried to process the sensation, he lifted his hand and quickly brought it down again.

Smack, smack, smack.

Over, and over, his hand landed on my round ass. My skin burned and my teeth dug into the large candy cane. I had no concept of time as I wriggled and whined on his lap. Tears streamed down my cheeks as my body flooded with sensation. Every smack made my clit throb and I was afraid my cunt was dripping onto his lap.

His hand moved from the rounded globes to the place where ass met thigh. I clenched my legs together, hoping he wouldn't know what a mess he was making of me. But he wouldn't allow it.

"What have we here?" His hand sank between my thighs, pushing my legs apart. He bent one at the knee and caught it under his leg, spreading me wide. Fingers tickled up my thigh and to the soaking place between.

"Such a naughty girl, getting off on your punishment." Leathery fingertips traced my soaking pussy before one finally, thankfully, slid inside. "Did you like that?"

"Yes," I mumbled the word around the candy in my mouth, riding his finger as he slowly pumped the large digit in and out of me.

"Then you're going to love this."

five

. . .

I WHINED as he withdrew his finger and smeared the creamy digit on the back of my leg. "Up you go."

He shifted us until I knelt on the ground, bent over the couch. My breasts and face shoved onto the cushions while my ass and pussy were exposed. Furry knuckles brushed down my slit before disappearing.

I didn't move. I wanted desperately to see what he was doing, but I was horny and unsatisfied and wouldn't survive it if he quit. And I knew without a doubt he would stop everything if I didn't keep my position.

There was a rustling and shifting and some soft sounds from the giant. I sat there with my cheek pressed to the fake leather, staring at the reflection of the tree lights in the window over the arm of the couch.

"Ah-ha!" It was a victorious sound. Then he was back, kneeling behind me. He pressed close, his cock hard and throbbing between us. He leaned over me, caging me in. The candy cane was removed from my mouth and tossed aside. "How are you doing, pretty?"

"Please," I begged, wiggling my ass against his hard dick. "Fuck me already."

"Such an impatient girl. There are hours left of the night and I plan on pleasuring you through every one of them." He pressed a kiss to my temple and pushed himself back up. "What would be the fun in fucking you when we've barely even started?"

He ground against me, his soft fur and hard cock teasing my soaked flesh. I was humping back against him the best I could, my arms still bound behind me and him pinning me in place. I was a panting, whining mess when he suddenly pulled away with a smack to my already burning ass.

"Naughty girl. Maybe I won't give you a present." Something hard and smooth was run up my leg to press against my swollen pussy. It circled my hole and I pushed back, desperate for anything to fill me. It slid inside slowly but easily. I was so wet I could fuck an eggplant without issue at this point. He fucked me with it slowly, so painfully slowly.

I writhed against it, trying for more friction. A hand came down onto my back to hold me in place. The pace of the item in my pussy didn't change. I could feel it as it pressed over every millimeter of my channel.

"So pretty, taking my candy cane." I jerked against his hand and fought to turn to look. He kept me in place but removed the item from inside of me.

"You are not fucking me with a candy cane. Do you know how horrible that is for the vagina?" A red and white phallic-shaped item appeared in front of my face. It was a basic torpedo-shaped toy. Not actual candy.

"Don't worry, pretty. I wouldn't do anything to risk this pretty pussy." He slid his hand down from my back to cup my cunt. He ground the palm against my hole as two fingers slid around and pinched my clit. "I have big plans for it. Are you ready for more?"

I nodded and relaxed back down to the couch. Now that yeast infections were off the table, I was ready for whatever he would give me. So long as it ended in an orgasm, I was game.

"That's my good girl." He gave a brief rub of my pussy with his soft, leathery hand before giving it a soft pat and pulling away. The sound of the vibrator turning on made me jump, but a gentle hand on my back pressed me down into position.

"Nothing you won't like." He promised as he slid the vibrating toy against my lips before sliding it into my painfully empty cunt. "Nothing that won't make you scream in pleasure."

"I don't scream," I said, my voice already shaking with impending orgasm. I'd been on edge for so long I knew it wouldn't take much to send me flying over the edge.

"You will tonight." It was a promise and a threat.

And I couldn't wait to see if he could make it come true.

six

. . .

MY THROAT WAS RAW. The monster went at me with the vibrator, sliding in and out of my dripping pussy before pressing it firmly against my clit. He repeated the cycle over and over as I panted and moaned and whined and begged. After a while, I could no longer recall if I was begging for release or begging for reprieve. It was all too much.

"That's my naughty, nasty girl," the monster crooned as he shoved me back to the edge before pulling the toy out of my cunt. "You're doing such a good job."

The vibrator turned off, and a whine escaped me. He'd been tormenting me for what felt like hours but still hadn't allowed me to come. I was on edge and ready to scream.

The candy-cane-colored toy appeared in front of my face, covered in my cream. I eyed the toy resentfully, hating I hadn't been allowed my release.

"Lick it." He moved the toy closer to my mouth and waited for me to open. "Taste yourself on my candy cane."

Dazed and exhausted, I obeyed. I opened my mouth for him to slip the toy inside, to fuck my mouth with the same bullet that had been torturing my pussy moments before. I'd never tasted myself before but the salty cum on the warm plastic wasn't as bad as I had expected.

"Look at you," he crooned. "I can't wait until it's my cock between those pretty pink lips."

He removed the toy and tossed it aside. I watched it roll under the chair, and made a mental note to get it before the kids got home. That was something I didn't want to explain.

"I'm not opposed to sucking your cock," I said, shifting on the couch to try to relieve the ache in my shoulders. "But I'm not doing it tied up."

"All you had to do was ask, pretty." There was a pull and a pop and the ribbon fell away. I pushed myself up onto my knees and rolled my shoulders.

"If I was better at asking things, I might not be divorced." It was partially true. My divorce was a result of terrible communication and some serious incompatibilities. I sucked at being direct in what I wanted, or needed, and he sucked at keeping a job and holding up his part of the marriage bargain.

"Should I tell you what you want, then?" He brushed my hair away from my face.

"How would you know what I want?" I sat back, resting my ass on my heels. The response was sarcastic, but the curiosity was genuine. He had sounded so confident when saying the words, I wondered if he had anything to back it up.

"Well, for one, I know you're dying for an orgasm."

I snorted. He'd been edging me for an hour. Of course, I was dying for an orgasm. It didn't take a genius to see that.

"I think you want someone who will take the time. I think you want to be worshiped, as you deserve." He offered a hand and pulled me to my feet when I accepted it. He pulled me close and wrapped his arms around me. For a moment, I allowed myself to accept the hug.

I was by no means a small person. I was five-seven and solidly mid-sized. It wasn't often I felt small, but I did in his embrace. The monster was seven feet tall, rounded and thick and soft. In his arms, I felt annoyingly safe and secure.

That thought unsettled me, and I pulled away. I did it slowly so he wouldn't guess at my upset. I should have known better.

"It's been a long time since someone has taken care of you. Let me be the one to give you what you need." He wrapped my hair in his fist and pulled my head back. I had no choice but to look at him. "Let me make you feel good."

I wanted to argue. I wanted to tell him I didn't need anyone to take care of me. I could and would make myself feel good. But his mouth was on mine and his tongue was invading and battling. His free hand slid down to my ass and used his grip on the bountiful flesh to pull me tight against him, his cock standing at attention between us.

I planted one hand on his arm, appreciating the soft flesh under the fur. The other hand slid between us to wrap around his dick. It was so thick my fingers barely brushed each other as I circled it. He throbbed under my grasp and let out a guttural moan. The sound was hoarse and broken and sent satisfaction zooming through me.

"Oh pretty, you shouldn't do that." He wrapped his hand around mine, preventing me from stroking him again.

"Turnabout is fair play," I argued, moving my other hand to wrap around the head of his cock and give it a tweak. He thrust forward into our joined hands.

"You're not the only one who hasn't had anyone take care of them in a long, long time." He gently pried my hands away from his cock and set them on his shoulders. He lifted me as though I weighed nothing, and I instinctively wrapped my legs around his wide hips, locking my feet at the base of his spine.

"Tell me you're ready for me." He said against my neck. His body was shaking and I couldn't help but do a slow grind against the cock trapped between us. "Tell me you can take me now."

"Fuck yes," I moaned, shifting my hips to try to help get him inside of me. "Fuck me already."

"As you wish, pretty." He worked a hand between us and used it to line his dick up with my hole. For some reason, I had expected a slow start, a gentle glide or shallow thrusts. Instead he pushed forward at the same time he slammed my hips down against him, fully seating himself inside of me.

I cried out, unable to stop the noise. He was so hard and hot and wide inside of me and my body was struggling to adjust, even as he began to move. He took a few stumbling steps and suddenly I was pressed between him and the wall. The wall was cool against my back, the monster hot against my front. His cock a brand inside of me.

"So fucking perfect," he groaned into my neck as he moved against me.

His fur was an entire sensory experience. It was soft and coarse, like a German shepherd's coat. And it was everywhere. From what I could tell, his penis, palms, and fingers were the only parts not covered in fur. Those were leathery and a little coarse, not unlike a dog's nose.

Those slightly rough hands held my ass tight against him. His fur brushed against my nipples and clit, offering a tease. I looked downward between our bodies and wished for a different position so I could see as he moved inside of me. All I could see was his furry green belly against my soft, pale one.

"What do you want, pretty?" My eyes flew to his. "You want something, tell me what you want."

"I want to see you. Us."

seven

. . .

THE WORDS WERE BARELY OUT of my mouth before I was pulled away from the wall. The monster spun around to look at the room and then settled on the chair. He sat me down on the seat and spread my legs wide until they hung over the arms before he dropped to his knees before me. Then he was back, his impossibly wide cock sliding into me.

It was the first time I'd gotten a good look at his penis. As he slid in and out, I appreciated the view of the green tool. It was the color of fresh kiwi with thick veins a few shades darker. It wasn't the longest dick I'd ever seen, but it was the widest I'd taken and it stretched my pussy to its limits.

"Beautiful."

I nodded my agreement, but when I glanced up, he wasn't staring at where our bodies joined. He was staring at me. His yellow eyes met mine, but I quickly looked away, unwilling to read the look there.

There was nothing sappy about this moment. It was dirty and physical and raw. I didn't want this monster sweet. I wanted him to fuck me until I couldn't feel my legs.

"Harder." I demanded, gripping his shoulders hard, digging in my nails into the flesh below all of the green fur. I planted a foot on the cushion of the chair and used it to give me the leverage I needed.

"Someone is hungry." The monster said, sliding his hand between us to circle two fingers against my clit. I gripped his wrist and pulled his hand away. My clit was wickedly over-stimulated and I wanted to enjoy the view a little while longer.

"That's not harder." I pointed out, releasing his wrist. "Fuck me."

"As my naughty girl demands."

He pulled me off the chair and onto the carpet. I was shoved onto my back and forced down as he scooped my legs up under his arms and gripped my soft thighs as he pressed them wide and toward my chest.

His cock was back in me, stretching me so wide as he slammed deep. The tip of his cock hitting the end of my vagina with every thrust. I hadn't had much sex since having a hysterectomy and I'd had no clue hitting the vaginal cuff would feel so damn good.

"Oh, my god." I moaned.

"God doesn't have anything to do with what you're feeling right now." The monster said, thrusting deep and circling his hips. "Who is making you feel so damn good right now?"

"You," I panted, tilting my hips into the thrust. "You are. Fuck." I tangled my hand in the fur on his arms and dug my nails into the flesh beneath.

"Come for me, pretty. Come for your imp." His thrusts became harder and more erratic. He was close. But so was I.

I reached one hand down between us to press and circle my clit. That was all it took. My pussy spasmed around him. He ground out something I couldn't understand before slamming deeper than ever. His cock throbbed inside of me and I could feel the spurts of cum paint my insides.

It was the hardest I'd ever come and even as I fought to catch my breath I wanted more.

eight

. . .

"WELL, this wasn't how I imagined my night going," the creature said, sliding down to lie beside me. He snagged his sack from the ground and produced a blanket. He tucked us under the fluffy white fabric before pulling me onto his chest.

I stacked my hands on his chest and pushed up so I could look him in the eye.

"What, exactly, were you expecting to happen here?"

His eyes shifted to the side, toward the Christmas tree that twinkled with white lights. He took a couple deep breaths before wrapping his arms around my waist and pressing me against him. His yellow eyes returned to me.

"I had planned to steal your Christmas. The gifts, the lights, the tree. All of it was going to come with me."

"What? Why?" I pushed against him, but he didn't let me up. Anger was a red flash through me and I needed to escape his arms.

"It's what I do." He shrugged, the movement shifting me against his chest. "It's what I've done for centuries. It's nothing personal."

"Feels pretty fucking personal to me." I struggled against him again. He released me, only to move his hands to my thighs, keeping me straddling his torso as I tried to get off of him.

"It wasn't. Your house was along Santa's path and it's my purpose in life to undo Christmas before Santa can deliver." I stared down at him.

Yes, I had just spent hours fucking a total stranger, a furry green monster with black nails and yellow eyes. The impossible was currently between my thighs. But the idea he was the anti-santa was absurd. Everyone knew Santa wasn't real.

"Bullshit."

"It's complicated." He slid me down until I was straddling his lap before he moved both of us until he was sitting up. He leaned against the couch and his hands cupped my bountiful ass.

"Then explain it to me." I ignored the slowly hardening dick beneath my butt as I stared him down. "And while you're at it, what is your name?"

"They call me The Imp, but my given name is Sully."

"Who calls you The Imp?"

"Santa and the other elves."

"Right, yeah, that's totally sane." Sully shifted me until his cock pressed between my gaping lower lips. I did my best to ignore it. I needed answers, not more sex.

"Santa isn't what you humans think of. The myth of delivering gifts to every kid is obviously false. But what he does is deliver the magic of Christmas. He travels the world dusting homes with holiday spirit."

I snorted. I couldn't help it. The whole thing sounded so absurd. Sully pinched my ass and I yelped and jumped against him.

"Do you want to hear this or not?"

I nodded, settling back down with his throbbing cock between my legs. He began pressing me down against him. I ignored it. I wanted the story.

"If Santa doesn't deliver gifts, what does he need elves for?"

"They gather the magic. It infuses the North Pole and has to be carefully gathered and packaged. It's terribly boring." He used his grip on my ass to slide me forward a little, dragging his cock between my over-sensitized lips. I gasped.

"That's what got me in trouble. The task was mind-numbingly dull and to amuse myself I started pulling pranks on the elves. At first, no one cared. It was silly things like nailing shoes to the floor or tying nightgowns to bed posts while they slept." Large hands slid me back and forth, teasing both of us. I uncrossed my arms and put my hands on his shoulders to get better balance as I began grinding against him of my own volition. "Mm, such a good fucking girl."

He leaned forward and pressed his mouth to mine. I allowed the kiss for a long moment before pushing him back and demanding the rest of the story.

"Things escalated until one Christmas I went riding with Santa to deliver Christmas cheer. While on the trip, I used some of the magic to swap out boring gifts for something more exciting." His yellow eyes met mine and twinkled with amusement. "I gave them the gift of pleasure. I gave them sex toys."

"Centuries ago?"

"Humans are so creative. They've been creating ways to fuck themselves and each other since the beginning of time." He urged me faster, pressed me down harder. I was so sensitive it was almost painful. The presence of pain only made the pleasure more intense.

"How did this prank lead you to stealing my Christmas?"

"Santa wasn't amused. The humans weren't amused. Christmas was chaos that year and the spirit of the holiday wasn't enough to keep the magic alive. It was almost the end of the holiday. Santa cursed me, turned me into this." He released my hip and gestured to himself. I looked over his green furry face and body, the firm slope of his stomach, the tree trunk thighs between my plush ones.

"I don't see a problem with this."

His smile was sad before he pressed a kiss to my forehead. "Thank you, pretty. But to the elves, this was the worst form they could imagine. Elves are only about five feet tall, they're pale and slender. Not a whole lot of sun in the North Pole most of the year. Being a seven-foot green monster made it easy for them to all shun me on sight.

"I decided if they were going to fear me and hate me, I'd give them something to hate. For centuries now I've been killing the holiday spirit for as many people as I could. Santa and the elves only survive so long as people believe in them. I wanted to end their existence."

I stopped grinding against him and stared at him. He was talking genocide. I clung to the last sentence.

"Wanted to? You don't anymore?"

"Right now, Devynn, the only thing I want is to stay here with you. This is the best I've felt in centuries. You bring me peace."

A little part of my heart melted at that. Then the

alarm bells started ringing in my head. He couldn't stay with me. That was insane.

"What do you mean stay with me? You can't stay with me!" I struggled away but he didn't let me go. "I have kids. How would I explain something like you to my children?"

"Devynn. Devynn, settle." Large hands soothed my back, pressing me to his broad, furry chest. "I cannot stay here past sunrise. With the dawn, I return to the North Pole with Santa and the elves and can't leave again until next Christmas. You will not have to explain the green monster to your children."

"Oh," That news didn't make me as relieved as I expected. I had no clue how I would go about explaining a giant green monster to my kids, but I also didn't want the night to end. Sully made me feel soft, beautiful, sexy, cherished. Things I hadn't felt in more years than I could remember. I didn't want to lose it.

"Will you miss me, pretty?" He pressed kisses to my neck, then another. I nodded into his chest, tears threatening and choking me.

"No, no, pretty. Don't cry over me."

"I can cry if I damn well want to cry." I snapped, annoyed at him, at myself, at the world.

"You can do whatever you want, pretty." His hands slid down my back, rough and furry and tickling against my skin. "But I'd rather make you feel good than make you sad."

His hands went back to my ass. Back to moving me against him. Back to grinding me down on his hard cock. I let him distract me but a part of me couldn't let it go. In a few short hours, he would be gone. And I would be alone.

Again.

nine

. . .

"STAY WITH ME, PRETTY." Sully said, adjusting me to where I was sitting on his cock. I rose up, allowing him to press against my opening. I wasn't sure if I was wet or relaxed enough to actually take him inside, but the tease was delicious. A groan rumbled from his throat and egged me on.

"Not yet, pretty. You're not ready yet." He moved with the swift power he'd been showing all night and switched our positions.

I was left sitting on the couch with his head and shoulders between my legs. He spread me wide and tugged my ass to the edge of the cushion so he could have easy access to my cunt. His tongue was slick and firm against me, circling my clit before sliding down to push into my tight hole. It went deeper and was wider than any tongue should be. He gently fucked me with it for long minutes before pulling out and moving back up to my swollen clit. He licked and flicked and sucked and nibbled on the sensitive bud, always keeping me on the edge but pulling back before I was able to go over.

"Fucking tease," I murmured, grabbing fistfuls of his hair to press his face harder against me. I had my heels planted on the edge of the couch as I humped up against his teasing face.

"I'll show you a tease," he grumbled into my pussy before pushing two broad, long fingers inside of me. I arched against him, against the invasion that burned so good. "I'm going to make you come until you beg me to stop. And then I'm going to flip you over and make you ride me."

I whimpered, moving against his hand and face. I was so close to the edge. This time, he took me over . And while I was still flying high, he brought me to the crest again. And again. I was panting and sobbing and begging for a reprieve, but still he pushed.

"That's it, pretty. My naughty girl. Keep coming for me."

"Can't. I can't. Please." I begged, trying to pull away from him. Trying to use my shaking legs to push him away.

"Have you had enough?" His grin was wicked.

"Yes, please, yes. Enough." He slowly slid his fingers from my body. They were coated white with me. He brought his hand up to his mouth and his red tongue peeked out to lap at my cream.

"You taste so sweet. I could eat you forever and never get enough."

I eyed him. He sat there on his knees with his pussy-coated fingers in his mouth. His green cock stood at attention between us and my mouth watered to get a taste of him. The brief feel he allowed me earlier made it clear it wasn't the same texture as human flesh and I wondered what his leathery penis would feel like under my tongue.

With shaking limbs, I pushed myself off the couch until I was again sitting on the floor. He was tall enough I didn't have to bend much to take him into my mouth. His cock was musky with the taste of both of us, and a little sweet. He groaned and tangled a hand in my hair. When he tried to pull me off, I sucked harder and took him deeper. His pull on me loosened and became a gentle push.

"Fuck me, pretty. You've got to stop or I won't last." I hummed, pleased by the idea he was so close to coming.

His cock was so wide my jaw ached as I sucked him as deep as I could. His leathery flesh offered some resistance to my movements at first, but between my spit and his pre-cum, it didn't take long before I was sliding up and down his length with ease.

"Pretty, be a good girl and stop now. I want inside of you." I shook my head as best as I could with a mouth full of cock. I wanted the taste of him on my tongue.

Plus, I was pretty sure I was never going to come again after all of the orgasms he forced me through. My legs still shook and my stomach and pussy occasionally fluttered with pleasure. No, I was good if we didn't have sex again, but I wanted to make him come.

"Devynn, stop." He pulled on my hair in earnest. I tightened my grip around the base of his cock and sucked hard. His cock sprung from a kind of slit in his pelvis and he didn't have any visible testicles. It was a bit strange and I kind of missed the ability to hold the weight of balls in my hand.

"Fuck. Fuck, fuck. You asked for this." He gripped my head in both hands and thrust forward a couple of times. His cock swelled almost impossibly. And he started coming. The hot taste of eggnog hit my tongue. Flooding my mouth with his flavored cum. He pulled back until only the tip remained in my mouth and I fought hard to swallow around the amount of cum he was ejaculating into my mouth.

I knew the average man only had a few milliliters of cum, but it felt like a cup of it was flooding my mouth and leaking out around his cock onto his fur and my chest. I swallowed and pulled away when he finally stopped spurting.

"I tried to warn you." He grumbled in that unused voice of his. He grabbed me under my arms and dropped me on the couch before leaving the room. I was sitting there trying to find the energy to get up and get cleaned up when he came back with a couple of towels. He used a damp one to gently wipe the cum off of me and the other to dry me off before helping me lay down on the couch under the blanket. He dropped the towels on the floor and crawled onto the couch with me.

It was a tight fit. Neither of us was a small being, but it was nice to be pressed against him and warm in his arms.

"Tell me something," he said, toying with my hair.

"Mmm?" I was so tired and content, I was on the edge of sleep.

"Why are you all alone? It's Christmas and you have stockings for three."

"I married a dick weasel. He has our children tonight." I snuggled into his furry chest. "I was pretty down about it too. Until you arrived to steal my Christmas tree."

We laid there in silence for a long time, his hand rubbing my back gently as the twinkle lights flashed. I was nodding off when he spoke again.

"Humans are idiots." He pressed a kiss to the top of my head. "If I had you, I'd never let you go."

Tears filled my eyes but I blinked them away. I wouldn't let myself cry over someone who wasn't, couldn't, stay. I was not going to let him break my heart. I stayed silent and was nodding off again when he whispered again. It was so quiet I nearly didn't catch it.

"I would give anything to keep you."

ten

· · ·

I WOKE to pounding on the door. The sun was streaming through the window, and I was momentarily disoriented until I realized I was on the couch.

Naked on the couch.

I sat up and looked around, searching for Sully. But there was no furry green monster, no large red sack, no sign of the ribbon he'd tied me up in or the towels or toys. If not for the fuzzy white blanket, I would have assumed the entire crazy encounter had been a dream.

After wrapping myself up in the blanket and grabbing my clothes from the floor, I rushed to the bedroom to put on a pair of sweats and a hoodie. My hair was a tangled mess that would need much more than a quick brush, so I tied it back in the messiest bun ever and called it good.

My ex was still pounding on the door when I returned. I pulled it open to three of the unhappiest faces I'd ever seen. Both of my children looked on the verge of tears. My ex's face was purple. He looked on the verge of a heart attack.

"What the hell took you so long?" Adam demanded. I ignored him in favor of giving my kids hugs and asking them to put their bags in their bedrooms.

"It's seven in the morning, Adam. I didn't expect you this early."

"Well those brats couldn't wait to get home. I cannot believe you're raising such terrible, ungrateful children."

"Goodbye Adam." I slammed the door in his face, unwilling to listen to him spew bile about me or my kids.

After getting them settled in with some cereal and a classic Christmas movie, I headed to the shower to get cleaned up. I could feel the dried cum all over me and needed a couple of moments to myself before I got the dad debrief and started our holiday.

A part of me was glad for the dried cum and the tangled hair. It was proof it happened. Proof Sully The Imp had been there and hadn't been a boozy dream. That someone had spent the night worshiping me. That I was still worthy of being worshiped.

I regretted falling asleep, I regretted the time I'd lost. I wished I would have asked if there was a way for him to stay. I wondered if he'd come back for me next year.

God, I hoped he would come back next year.

eleven

. . .

"MOM, why do you look so nice? It's bedtime." I brushed the hair away from my daughter's sweet face and gave her a smile.

"Sometimes I just like to look pretty. Are you ready for Christmas tomorrow?"

She nodded, yawning wide.

"Are you sure Santa is going to come? He didn't come to Dad's and daddy said he isn't real." I would never get over my anger at my ex for failing to give the kids a real Christmas the year before. Not only did he not bother with the tree and stockings, but he had the audacity to tell our elementary aged children Santa was a myth. I still shook with rage when I thought about it too hard.

"I'm sure Santa will be here." I brushed a kiss to her forehead and helped adjust the blankets to her liking. "Now you need to go to sleep so he can come and bring you your gifts."

"But what if he forgets about us again? Or thinks we're at Daddy's house because we were last year?"

"Remember, we sent him the note with your

lists? I'm sure it will be fine." I got off the bed and turned off the lamp, ready to make my escape.

There were only three more hours until midnight and Christmas and I had much to get ready. Oh, the presents were wrapped and ready to be put under the tree. The stockings were hanging and waiting to be filled. Cookies and milk were on display under the tree, which once again twinkled with white lights.

I was prepared for Christmas to arrive, more so than I'd ever been before. I'd been more excited for the holiday than either of my children.

After I was certain both children were fast asleep, I finished getting ready.

I had no way of knowing if the Imp would return for me or not. I'd spent the year telling myself it had been a magical night and I was lucky to have it. But I'd never gotten over the feelings he'd given me.

Sure, I'd tried to date. But no one made me feel as beautiful or wanted as Sully. I'd never even made it to bed with anyone, because there simply wasn't the spark I'd felt with the green monster. For those few hours last Christmas, I'd been exactly the person I always wanted to be and loved exactly how I deserved to be. How was I supposed to settle for anything less?

All year long, I'd tried telling myself it was a single night of magic and I had to move on. But the closer we got to the holidays, the more I thought about Sully and wanted him. I didn't care if I had to come up with a way to explain a furry green monster man to my kids. I wanted him with me all the time and I was hoping this year we'd be able to come up with some way for him to stay.

I refused to accept the possibility he wouldn't

come back to me. The rational part of my brain told me he probably never thought about me, that despite what he'd said, it probably was his game to seduce a new person every Christmas. Why else would he have a sack packed with toys?

But I couldn't believe it. I didn't want to believe it.

When the clock struck midnight, I was waiting for him. I stood in the living room in my red lace bra and panties, candy cane stockings, and white silk robe and waited for him. I'd wrapped my long black hair up in a braided crown to prevent the snarls and tangles I'd sustained last Christmas.

By twelve-thirty, I was sitting on the couch trying not to nod off. Sometime around one, I lost the fight. I curled up on the couch under the white blanket that was all that remained from my night with Sully. I told myself it was stupid for my heart to break over someone that was impossible, but my heart had no interest in listening.

twelve

. . .

"WAKE UP, PRETTY." The words were a whisper that matched the ghost of a touch across my bare shoulder. I sighed and snuggled deeper into the pillows, not wanting to wake up and lose the dream. It was one I'd had a number of times over the year since my magical night with the Imp. He came to me in my sleep and woke me up to pleasure me over and over again. I'd wake up panting and empty and so frustrated and horny. I'd burned the motor out of the candy cane bullet vibrator I'd pulled out from under the chair.

"Come on, be a good girl for me." When a hand fisted in my hair, my eyes flew open. He was there!

Sully knelt on the ground beside the couch. He was green, furry, naked, and grinning at me as he tugged my head back and exposed my neck to his lips and teeth. I shoved him back to get a look at him and make sure he was real.

"You're here!" I launched myself off of the couch at him.

"Did my naughty girl miss me?" His arms closed around me and he hugged me close to his chest. His face buried in my hair and he took a deep breath. I didn't even care if he was sniffing me. I was smelling him too. I was getting high on his cinnamon, cloves, and peppermint scent. His fur was softer than I remembered and I couldn't help but bury my hands and face in it.

"I didn't know if you'd come back." The tears didn't escape, but they pressed close to the surface. I wasn't even entirely sure why I was crying. My rational brain knew it was insane to feel so much after one encounter, a year before, but I couldn't stop myself.

"I told you I would." He wrapped his hand around the back of my neck and pulled me away. "Over and over, all year long, I promised you I'd be back." His yellow eyes were intent on mine. They bore into me and meaning sunk in.

"I thought they were dreams."

"Dreaming of me?" He brushed a kiss to my forehead. "I came to you every chance I could in the only way I was allowed. Magic can do powerful things but it also sets annoying limitations."

"At least we have tonight." I pressed my lips to the line of his mouth, his own lips so thin they barely existed. "At least I have you now."

His tongue swept out. The kiss was messy and wet. I buried my hands into the fur of his chest and shoulders, holding him in place as I fell into the kiss. I couldn't get enough of him. I wanted to drown in him.

"Shhh, pretty. Slowly." He pressed me back against the side of the couch and looked me over. A wicked smile slowly spread over his green face. Yellow eyes focusing on the bow between my breasts.

"You're such a pretty present and I'm going to take my time unwrapping you this time." He boosted me until I was back on the couch, my legs spread wide to accommodate his broad form. Warm hands slid up over my shins, knees, up to my thighs. He used the grip to spread them impossibly wide. My muscles ached as I fought to keep the position. I wanted to hear him call me a good girl in that scratchy, unused voice of his.

He shifted, lowering himself until he could press a kiss to the inside of my thigh by my knee. Then another, higher. And another. A hot trail of kisses up my leg that led to the flesh already wet and throbbing between them.

His mouth pressed to my mound, over my underwear. A firm kiss dulled by the lace. The kiss was followed by a long lick of his tongue, from hole to clit. I whined and wriggled against the grip he had on my thighs. It felt good, but it wasn't enough. I wanted his mouth on me.

Normally, I would appreciate a slow build up, but I could hear the mantle clock ticking away the seconds. There were mere hours until morning and I didn't want to waste a moment of our night together.

"More," I demanded. It caused Sully to chuckle against me, the sound sending vibrations across my clit. "Stop teasing me already!"

I moved my hands to the bows at my hips but he slapped them away.

"I told you, I'm going to take my time unwrapping you." He sunk his teeth into my thigh, a dull pain that distracted from the throbbing nearby. "Now be a good girl and take what I give you. Unless you want me to pull the ribbon out already."

My entire body flushed. I'd never been tied up before last Christmas and it had been the hottest thing I'd ever experienced. The feeling of helplessness had been heady. I wondered if the touch of fear would still be there.

But no, I wanted to be able to touch him in return. I wanted to make him feel good too. Something I wouldn't be able to do if my hands were bound.

"I'll be good," I promised as I tangled my hands into the fur of his shoulders. "But please, I need more."

His eyes dropped to my core, where I couldn't help but thrust toward him. The gusset of the panties was already so wet, dark with a combination of his mouth and my wetness.

"Don't worry, pretty. I'll give you everything you need." His head dropped to lick over me again. "Just give me a moment to enjoy my treat. It's been a long year and while your dreams are a lovely place to be, nothing beats the real thing."

Fingers found the edge of my panties where it met my thigh and slid beneath. The touch of his rough skin on my damp flesh had me jerking in place. I needed more of his touch.

"Please," I begged, ready to do anything for what I needed. "Touch me already."

He bit my thigh again, harder this time. I yelped but forced myself to remain still, afraid if I moved; the fingers gently brushing against my lips would stop.

"Patience," he demanded, licking the wound he'd just inflicted. His mouth moved over to lick along the seam of my thigh. The feeling of it so close to my bare flesh was almost too much. I bit my lip and clenched my fingers on his shoulders. I shook with the effort to stay still and accept what he was willing to give.

His fingers pulled away, and I whined, thrusting to chase his touch. It was a relief when his hand went to the bow at my hip. A sharp tug and the ribbon came loose. He repeated the move on the other side and then pulled the panties forward until I was laid bare to him.

"Such a pretty pussy," he murmured, brushing the back of his fingers across the damp flesh. My legs shook. My teeth cut into my lip with almost bruising force as I fought the urge to demand he touch me again.

His hand moved to frame me. His thumbs spread my lips wide. A dark green tongue flicked out to lick his lips as he stared down at me. His yellow eyes almost glowed with unholy light as his head dipped to finally, fucking finally, run his tongue up the exposed flesh. His groan matched my moan when the lick turned into a gentle suck at my swollen clit.

"You taste so fucking good." His words spoken into my flesh and followed by another lick. Another suck. I moved my hands to cup his head and keep him in place. A part of me was worried he would take it as a demand and tie me up again, but he didn't slow down as his tongue worked me up.

It took a pathetically short time before I was writhing and doing my best to muffle my moans.

"I want to hear you," Sully demanded, sucking hard on my clit. My hand flew to my mouth as I bit back a moan. "Let me make you scream."

"Can't," I panted the word behind my hand before dropping it away. "My kids are upstairs. We can't wake them up."

"Then I guess you'll have to be quiet." His

smirk was evil as he pulled my panties out from underneath me and balled them up. "Open."

"Oh, there's no way." I shook my head, absolutely not opening my mouth for what had to be soaked panties.

"Be a good girl for me and open up." He held my face, fingers pressing against my jaw. "We don't want to risk waking the children and putting an end to our fun, do we?"

He pressed the damp material against my mouth and pulled it tight. He used the ribbons that made up the sides to tie the underwear in place. I glared at him but didn't move to undo it. He was stronger and faster. And I had no doubt it would only end up with me tied and bent over his lap again.

And while I wasn't entirely against the idea, it wasn't what I wanted. Not right then.

"Now, where was I?" He licked his lips again before ducking his head to put his mouth to me. This time, his fingers followed. The thick, leathery digits pushed into me and stretched me wide. My grip on his head tightened, the mix of pain and pleasure sending me straight to the edge. A twist, a curl, a suck and I was there, flying off the cliff into orgasm. His free hand flew to my mouth, muffling the moans that escaped past the gag.

"That's my good girl. Keep coming for me." He sucked my clit hard, pressing the tips of his fingers against my g-spot. "I'll never get enough of how you taste."

In a flash, he pulled away. He gripped my thighs and yanked me off of the couch before flipping around to bring me down to the carpet. The show of strength as he threw my plus-sized body around had me clenching on nothing.

"Quiet now," he said, moving over me. He lined his cock up with my hole and sank deep with one thrust. His hand slapped over my mouth just in time to muffle the scream at the feel of him stretching me impossibly wide. I had forgotten how big he was, how impossible the stretch felt as he filled me.

"I'm going to stay like this all night long," he promised, slowly pulling out. I could feel every ridge of his cock against my walls at the impossibly slow glide. He stopped with the tip inside of me before slamming deep again. I arched and moaned. My nails dug into the carpet at my hips.

"I'm going to fuck you until your legs stop working and you can't remember your name anymore." Another painfully slow withdrawal and punishing thrust in. "I'm going to fuck you until the only thing you can think of is me."

He kept up that slow, punishing rhythm, driving me absolutely out of my mind. Between the gag and his hand pressing against my mouth, I stopped trying to hold back my sounds as I sped back toward orgasm.

"Do you know how infuriating it was when I couldn't reach you? How many nights you didn't let me into your dreams and I was left alone with only the memory of the taste and feel of you?"

I wanted to tell him I was sorry, to beg for forgiveness. To ask him to stay. I wanted so much to keep him.

I hugged my arms around his shoulders and pulled him down to me until I could bury my face in his neck. My legs wrapped around his hips and held him to me, telling him with my body how sorry I was for leaving him alone.

Tears welled in my eyes, but I blinked them

away. My poor monster was so alone. It wasn't fair. He'd played one bad prank and was forced out on his own for centuries. I was certain I wasn't the first woman he'd found comfort in but every part of me wanted to be the last. I wanted to give him everything he needed.

Hands tangled in my hair and tugged. The gag at my mouth came loose. Sully pulled away far enough to remove the panties from my mouth and toss them aside. He brushed my damp hair from my face with his thumbs and stared into my eyes.

"I won't tell you not to cry for me, pretty, because I know you'll just yell at me again. But it really is okay. What you give me is enough to keep me sane." His mouth slanted over mine. The kiss tender as he started to move inside of me again. The punishing pace switching to a slow, gentle glide. We moved together, wrapped around each other. Even with the ticking of the clock marking down the seconds until morning, there was no rushing. We were taking the moment for ourselves.

This time my climax was a slow build, a warm flush across my body and kindling deep in my belly. It washed over me in gentle waves rather than a hard crash. I came on a sigh as Sully thrust deep one final time and twitched inside of me as he spilled his warm cum into me.

He rolled us until I was laying on top. When I tried to roll off to lay next to him, he held me tight, keeping me in place on his chest.

"I'll crush you," I argued. It was unconvincing. I laid my head on his chest just above his pounding heart as I said the words, content to lay wrapped in his warmth.

"Don't be silly," he pressed a kiss to the top of my head. There was some wiggling and shifting and then the soft blanket I'd left balled on the floor fell over us. "Rest, I'm not done with you."

I was already drifting off to sleep, my body warm and comfortable, wrapped up with my furry green monster.

thirteen

. . .

I AWOKE WITH A START. It took me a moment to gain my bearings and sort out what had woken me. There, a thump upstairs. One of the kids?

The blanket tangled around my legs as I struggled to climb off of the slowly awakening monster beneath me. I was naked in the living room with a furry green monster and one of my kids could come downstairs at any movement.

"Wake up!" I hissed, shoving Sully with both hands before climbing to my feet. I twirled around the room, looking for my robe. There was no time to put my underwear back on, those damn ribbons weren't easily managed.

"Sully, you have to hide. My kids." I looked at the clock on the mantle, confused at how we'd slept so long, but it was only three o'clock.

"Devynn," Sully's scratchy voice did nothing to soothe my nerves as I snatched up the abandoned panties and balled them in my hand. There. My robe was on the couch.

I shoved my arms in the silky material and shoved the lace scraps into the pocket. I quickly tied the robe and was tugging on my socks to put them back in place when Sully came up behind me with his hands on my hips.

"Settle. It's not your kids." I twirled around, my heart still racing at the idea of being caught with him.

Stupid. I was so stupid. What had I been thinking, having sex with him in the living room? My bedroom was right there. We could have been in my room with the locking door instead of naked on the living room floor. What if one of them had come down while we were sleeping? How could I ever explain?

"Devynn, you need to calm down." He released me but was back a moment later, wrapping me up in our white blanket. "We have a visitor."

I spun around in his arms, trying to process his words. We have a visitor?

"Hello Sullivan. Long time no see." The voice came from my fireplace. The fire was banked, but the coals went instantly cold just before two black boots landed in the ash. I watched in confusion and amazement as a large white man wearing a red suit bent down and ducked out of my fireplace.

"Devynn, a pleasure." The man was round, with a grey and white beard that covered most of his face and white hair that curled out from under his had. He had big blue eyes but they didn't twinkle like they did in every Santa picture I'd ever seen. No, these eyes were cool.

"What?" I asked him before looking at Sully, whose face was very neutral. "What?"

"Devynn, meet Santa Claus." His voice was even, toneless.

Right. Okay.

Santa fucking Claus was standing in my living room and I was wearing little more than a blanket and smelled of sex. At least I had gotten my underwear off the floor.

"Come to ruin my life some more?" Sully asked, "Sense me getting a moment of joy and decide we couldn't have that?"

His tone was harsh but his movements were gentle as he released me and moved to stand between me and the myth standing beside my fireplace. I pulled the blanket tighter around me and moved to stand by his side. I chose to ignore the sour look he shot me.

"You were such a terrible elf," the large man grumbled. "Always so self-centered and surly. It was a wonder you lasted as long as you did. But no, I'm not here for you. I'm here for her."

Santa's gaze shifted to me. Beside me, Sully stiffened before he wrapped an arm around my waist and pulled me closer. I met Santa's icy blue gaze and waited for him to explain.

While a part of me was still freaking out Santa fucking Claus was in my living room, Sully's cold reaction had me worried. I knew there were centuries of hard feelings there, but I didn't want him to further anger the man and be taken from me.

"She doesn't need you." Sully growled.

"You don't know what she needs." Santa's voice was calm and cold. His eyes never left me as he dismissed my monster so cooly.

"And you do?" I challenged him. For all I knew, he could see into my soul and knew exactly what I needed. But I didn't like the way he was dismissing Sully, talking down to him. I honestly didn't like him in my space uninvited. I didn't like him taking up precious minutes that could be spent loving the person beside me.

"Need? Maybe not," Santa said, strolling over to

the tree and grabbing a cookie from the plate sitting underneath it. "But I know what you want. And I could give it to you."

My eyes slid to Sully. He stood silent and still beside me, his arm a hard band behind my back. He didn't look at me, but I could see his jaw working as he ground his teeth together.

"How?" Because the only thing I really wanted was to have Sully. But I couldn't have a furry green monster as a husband. And if I did, it would just cause more complications than anything. How do you explain to a six-year-old he could never tell anyone about the monster sleeping in mom's bed?

"I'm fucking Santa Claus," he shrugged. "I can do anything I want."

"Bullshit." Sully said, glancing down at me before turning to glare at the man casually crunching cookies beside the tree.

"Are you sure you want him?" Santa asked me, an eyebrow cocked so high it disappeared under the brim of his red and white hat.

"Absolutely." No hesitation. But then– "I can't, though. The children…"

"I'll take care of it." Santa finished off the cookie in his hand and dusted them together, sending crumbs falling down onto his round belly. "Come along, Sullivan. We have things to do."

"No," the word was firm. It left no room for argument or conversation. I was having none of it.

I turned to face him. His arm fell away from me and he crossed them over his wide chest, resting on the curve of his belly. His eyes were bright, and he looked ready for a fight.

"Sully," I started. He immediately cut me off.

"No, you don't know the kind of game he's playing. He might seem like he's offering you what you want but it could ruin everything. I can't risk it. I can't risk losing what we have."

"What do we have? A few hours once a year? Is that really enough?"

Tears welled in my eyes and he broke. His eyes went soft. He reached out to cup my face and used a thumb to wipe a tear away as it slid down my cheek. He stood there staring at me for a long minute, not saying a word.

"This is touching and all but I don't have all night. It's rather a busy one, you might recall. Are we doing this or not?"

I spun around to look at the old man who could either give me everything I wanted or ruin my entire life. The blanket fell to the floor, and I stood there in my thin white robe. I clutched the collar tight over my chest and glared at him.

"What, exactly, are you doing?"

"Making your wish come true."

Oh, he was infuriating. "That's not an answer."

He sighed; a big, obnoxious sound that made me want to release my lapels and grab onto his to shake him.

"Sullivan has spent centuries trying to ruin Christmas, ever since that disastrous year with the sex toys. He's been a pain in my ass, a cause of anxiety for the other elves. Until last year. Since last Christmas, he's been quiet in his sad little cave. He hasn't done one thing to cause me or my elves any issue. He's just been focused on you. This year, the second he could, he was back down your chimney."

Santa looked over at the glowering green guy and rolled his eyes. I wanted to slap him. Sully looked close to punching him and I wouldn't have stopped him.

"You do something to him, and I'm happy to grant your Christmas wish if it means permanently removing this thorn from my side." He looked to Sully now. "You know I can't make you human, not fully. But I can give you a human appearance."

"No." Sully said. I whirled around to look at him, astounded by his refusal.

"But why?"

"I'm not going to watch you die. I'm not going to sit idly by and watch you age and decay. It would be worse than never seeing you again." He reached out and toyed with a strand of hair that had come loose.

"Oh, don't be stupid." Santa said from behind me. "There are ways around that. Ways we can discuss in the future when the time comes. Now are we doing this?"

"I don't trust him," Sully said.

"It's your choice, Sully I won't ask you to do it." I stepped close and pressed my lips to the thin line of his mouth. "But I can't have only one night a year. I won't survive it."

With my heart breaking, I left the room and didn't look back.

fourteen

. . .

"BEST. CHRISTMAS. EVER!" My daughter Bethany sat in the wrapping paper wasteland with a broad grin on her face. She carefully cradled her new phone in one hand and sifted through a trio of cases for it with the other hand.

She grinned up at me and I tried to grin back. It was hard. So fucking hard. I wish I had someone I could talk to about my broken heart, but who would I tell? I'd never told Amy about my encounter with the monster last Christmas. And even if I had, she never would have understood. Love at first sight wasn't a real thing. There was no reason my heart should break over two random encounters. But I couldn't deny it was what was happening.

"Mom, do we have any batteries?" My son held out a fresh-from-the-box toy.

"You know we do," I assured him, taking the toy and stealing a moment to brush my hand over his soft curls. "I'll go pop some in."

I left my kids to their new treasures and headed into the kitchen to find the screwdriver and batteries. I'd get the toy fired up and then start breakfast. The day would go on and I would pull it together to give my kids the happy mom they deserved.

I was halfway down the hall when the doorbell rang. I stopped, wondering who the heck was ringing the bell on Christmas morning. We never had anyone over in the morning and we spent the afternoon at my parent's house. It wouldn't be my ex. He had only seen the kids a handful of times in the last year after the debacle of last Christmas.

Did people carol on Christmas day?

The door rang again and Ryan ran out of the living room in his red and green jammies, making a beeline to the door. We were still working on not opening the door to strangers, and I watched in horror with a 'no' halfway up my throat when he flung it open.

"Merry Christmas!" He shouted to whoever was on the other side. "Did you bring presents?"

"Ryan!" I snapped, rushing down the hall toward him. "Remember what we said about opening the door? I'm so sorry."

I looked out at the man standing on my doorstep and then froze. The man there was an absolute giant. Tall, wide, with a clearly soft belly. He has pale green eyes, longish black hair, and a plush mouth curved up into a smile as he looked down at Ryan.

His clothes were simple. Just a pair of jeans and a soft-looking red sweater under an open black wool coat. Everything about him seemed friendly and inviting.

I had never seen him before in my life. I was getting ready to shoo him off, not trusting anyone knocking on my door at the best of times. And then he spoke.

"I did," he said, handing two bright red bags to Ryan. "One for your sister too."

I froze in my tracks. His face may be new, but the rough, unused voice haunted my dreams for over a year and I'd never forget it.

Ryan started reaching for them, then stopped to look at me. I nodded, giving him the okay to take them. I stood completely speechless as he thanked the man for the presents and ran off with them to the living room, screaming to his sister there were more gifts.

Cold air streamed into the hallway as I stared at the human-looking man in my doorway. Human and sexy. Oh, he was so incredibly sexy.

"Invite me in?" Sully asked, shoving his hands into his pockets. That made me laugh and broke the shell of shock.

"Since when do you need an invitation?" I reached out and pulled the door wide before stepping aside to let him in.

"Since you told me to leave." He stepped inside and pulled the door from my hands to close it behind him. We stood there in awkward silence, just staring at each other.

"Fuck, I can't take this. I need to touch you." He reached out and fisted a hand in my hair, bending to kiss me. It was brief. A hard press of lips to mine before he raised his head and stared down at me with those new green eyes. A part of me immediately missed the nearly glowing yellow orbs he used to have.

"Sorry, I just-" He shook his head and released my hair before driving both of his hands into his own hair. "Tell me I can be here."

"I don't even understand how you're here."

"Christmas magic." He shrugged, shoving his

hands back into his pockets. I crossed mine under my breasts, needing to keep myself from reaching out to him. I was acutely aware of my kids a room away. The action figure I was supposed to be powering up dug into the side of my boob, but I welcomed the discomfort. It was a sign it was real. This was actually happening.

"I couldn't take it when you walked away." He reached out, dropped his hand. "The idea of never being with you again was too much. So I took the fat man up on his offer. It's not all sorted. I'm still physiologically an elf with an elf lifespan. A lifespan that spans centuries instead of decades. But it's something we have time to figure out."

"But you said-"

"I know what I said." He did touch me this time, grabbing both of my arms and pulling me close to him. Not quite all of the way into his body, but close. There was a matter of inches between my chest and his. "It doesn't matter. I'll do anything to have you."

I uncrossed my arms, dropping the toy to the floor as I reached up to grab his lapels and pull him down into me. My lips met his in a hard press. The pain from the night before collided with my joy and relief at having him there and burst out of me on a sob.

"You're serious? You're really here." I muttered the word between kisses.

"I'm here. And I'm not going anywhere." He pressed his lips to mine, his tongue swept out to the seam of my mouth. I was about to open to him when the words hit me.

"Oh my god, how am I going to explain you to my kids? You can't stay here! They'd never understand."

Sully laughed. It was a loud, full sound that filled the hallway. It lit up his face and made me want to smile. But I couldn't. Because I had a fucking elf standing in my hallway saying he was staying forever and two kids in the living room waiting for breakfast and it was just insane.

"Aw pretty," he pulled me into a big hug that was soft and warm and filled with his laughter. "Your panic is adorable. When I said I wasn't going anywhere I didn't mean I was moving in. I understand. Part of the deal I made with the elfish overlord was making sure I had a place to live and a way to get by in the human world. It'll be okay."

I sagged into him, so relieved he had thought of my kids and hadn't presumed I would take him in. Yet perversely, it made me wish I could. It made me wish I could keep him with me.

"I have a six-month lease on an apartment nearby. We can reevaluate the situation then." He pressed a kiss to my head and pulled me away. "I'll tell you now, I intend to move in with you. Be with you. I want to be your everything and I won't be content to do it from a distance forever."

"We'll figure it out," I promised him. I stepped back and took his hand in mine. "Now, can I trust you to not destroy any more ornaments if I let you near my tree?"

"That damn glass ball," he shook his head but he couldn't hide the smile or the glint in his eye as he stepped to me. "I can't believe that's what got me caught."

"I still have it, you know. The pieces of that ornament." I felt silly saying it but a part of me really wanted him to know.

"What? Why?" His brows drew in and I reached up to smooth them out again.

"It was one of the few reminders I had of the best Christmas I'd ever had."

"Best Christmas ever, huh?"

"Well, until now." I pressed my lips to his before picking up the abandoned toy and starting down the hall. I smiled at him as I moved backward toward the kitchen and my task there.

"This is definitely the best Christmas ever."

author's note

This is a monster romance. Humans will be getting it on with with a monster.

But if you're going to stick around please be aware of the following:

This book contains a terrible father figure, breaking & entering, a brief moment of dub-con, spanking, light bondage, edging, forced orgasms, use of gags.

The bondage performed in this book is not a safe method and the author discourages use of curling ribbon for your playtime. Please make smart and educated bondage decisions.

If you feel I am missing anything please reach out to me at authorsabrinacross@gmail.com and let me know. A complete list can be found at www.sabrinacross.com

acknowledgments

While this book may be dedicated to my Twitter friends made over the years, there are three people in particular who I can firmly place the blame of its existence on. @SashaDevlin, @AllieIsWriting and @bandherbooks have made my holiday season a joy for years with the sexy grinch memes and jokes and horror. Long before any of them knew who I was, I would follow along and secretly agree that the furry green monster with a dad bod was mighty sexy. I don't know if you'll be pleased or horrified but this one is for you.

As always, I have to thank Brittany, whose long-suffering patience with me as I plot and change and write is the stuff of legends and no books would ever exist if I didn't have her in my corner. Plus, the endless task of reminding me that commas exist and that I cannot possibly start every single sentence in every single paragraph with the word "I."

Nicole, Mia, Ellie, Michaela, Paondel, Sylvia & everyone else who hangs out on Discord with me, y'all are invaluable. Thanks for kicking my butt and cheering me on and all of the general shenanigans. You make my day brighter in so many ways.

Devynn, thanks for letting me use your name. It's a pretty fantastic one. I hope you love it.

Most importantly, to my readers, thank you. I wouldn't be able to keep doing this without you. Please know that every post, tag, message, or review means everything to me. Thank you, thank you, thank you.

about the author

Sabrina Cross (she/her) is a neurospicy 80's baby from the middle of nowhere Michigan, where she still lives with her cat. She came into her monster romance era early when she fell in love with Beast from the 1997's X-Men animated series. After discovering sentient object romance in early 2023, Sabrina decided to embrace what she calls her 'Hold My Beer' style of writing and gave into the lifelong dream of being an author. When not writing weird monster/sentient object smut, Sabrina can be found hanging out on social media (@authorsabrinacross), reading, or hoarding office supplies.

also by sabrina cross

Yarn & Monsters Series

A True Love Spell Gone Wrong...

When four friends perform a true love spell, things go terribly wrong. Now they're locked into a deal with the devil and have only a year to find love and happiness or their souls are destined to face the flames. Armed with a demon guardian; Clover, Jasmine, Fern, and Violet are determined to beat the devil and save themselves. Except, this curse might be the best thing that's ever happened to them.

Corny: A F/F Candy Corn Romance

A True Love Spell Gone Wrong…

A Demon Fairy Godmother?

Her very soul on the line. Can Clover still find true love or is she destined to face the flames alone?

Snuggle: A M/F Demon Teddy Bear Romance

A True Love Spell Gone Wrong…

Jasmine is too busy to go to Hell and she's definitely too busy for demon antics. But when her demon "Fairy Godmother" shows up, everything is on the line. Does she have what it takes to get out of the Devil's bargain or is she doomed to face the flames?

Tangled: A M/F Friends-To-Lovers Sentient Object Romance

A True Love Spell Gone Wrong…

Fern is going to Hell. Not metaphorical Hell but actual, physical Hell. But there's one thing she needs to do before she goes. An item she desperately needs to scratch off the bucket list. And she's hoping the demon sent to guard her will be willing to help her out.

Knotted: A M/F Demon Werewolf Romance

A True Love Spell Gone Wrong…

Violet was no witch but that didn't stop her from trying to use magic to find love. When the spell backfired and left her and her friends bound in a deal with the devil, Violet vowed to find a solution. Now, with less than two months until the deal comes due and zero leads, she's facing the fire. The fire comes early in the form of a great black beast in her bed. Does Violet find the love she's been looking for or does Hell claim her soul?

Light Me Up

He was the first man to ever turn me on. When he flipped my switch and lit me up that first time, I knew he was it for me. There would never be another.

Pounded by the Pommel Horse

Elena loves being on top. When the elite gymnast is challenged to defeat her gym rival on the pommel horse, she's up for the task. But is she up for the ride when the pommel horse shapeshifts into a man? A very, very naked Man?

Christmas with the Monster

He's Got a Package for Her... Devynn expected her first holiday without her kids to be difficult. But nothing could have prepared her for what she found under the tree just after midnight.With the help of his magic sack, the furry, green giant promises Devynn all kinds of pleasure. But would one night with the Christmas monster ever be enough?

Sentient Pen15 from Outer Space

Liam had spent a lot of his childhood obsessed with the legends of the local mines. The abandoned tunnels underground had driven dozens of workers insane and young Liam was desperate to get to the bottom of it. But he found more than he bargained for down there.

Infected by parasitic space mold, Liam has held himself away from relationships for years. When things spark between him and the girl next door, he has no choice but to reveal the truth: his manly appendage is also the bane of his existence.

The Glory Whole Package

Never Piss Off a Witch.

It is a hard-learned lesson and one I may never complete. The endless boredom of my curse is only broken by analyzing the people who use me.

Today I break my silence for the first time and while it might lead to a Happily Ever After, it will never be mine. Not until I've paid for my crimes and earned the forgiveness of the only person I've ever loved.

Getting Railed

"Welcome to Retro Whimsy!"

I hadn't planned on buying anything when entering the new vintage store during my lunch break but somehow found myself leaving with a toy train set.

What could have been written off as an impulse purchase became so much more when those trains come to life.

Now I'm stuck dealing with the consequences of a god curse and deciding if I have what it takes to help break it.

www.ingramcontent.com/pod-product-compliance
Lightning Source LLC
Chambersburg PA
CBHW020735310726
48969CB00003B/843